Cambridge Early Years

Mathematics

Learner's Book 3B

Alison Borthwick & Cherri Moseley

Contents

Note to parents and practitioners   3

Block 3: Caring for ourselves and the world   4

Block 4: Then and now   18

Acknowledgements   32

Note to parents and practitioners

This Learner's Book provides activities to support the second term of Mathematics for Cambridge Early Years 3.

Activities can be used at school or at home. Children will need support from an adult. Additional guidance about activities can be found in the **For practitioners** boxes.

Children will encounter the following characters within this book. You could ask children to point to the characters when they see them on the pages, and say their names.

The Learner's Book activities support the Teaching Resource activities. The Teaching Resource provides step-by-step coverage of the Cambridge Early Years curriculum and guidance on how the Learner's Book activities develop the curriculum learning statements.

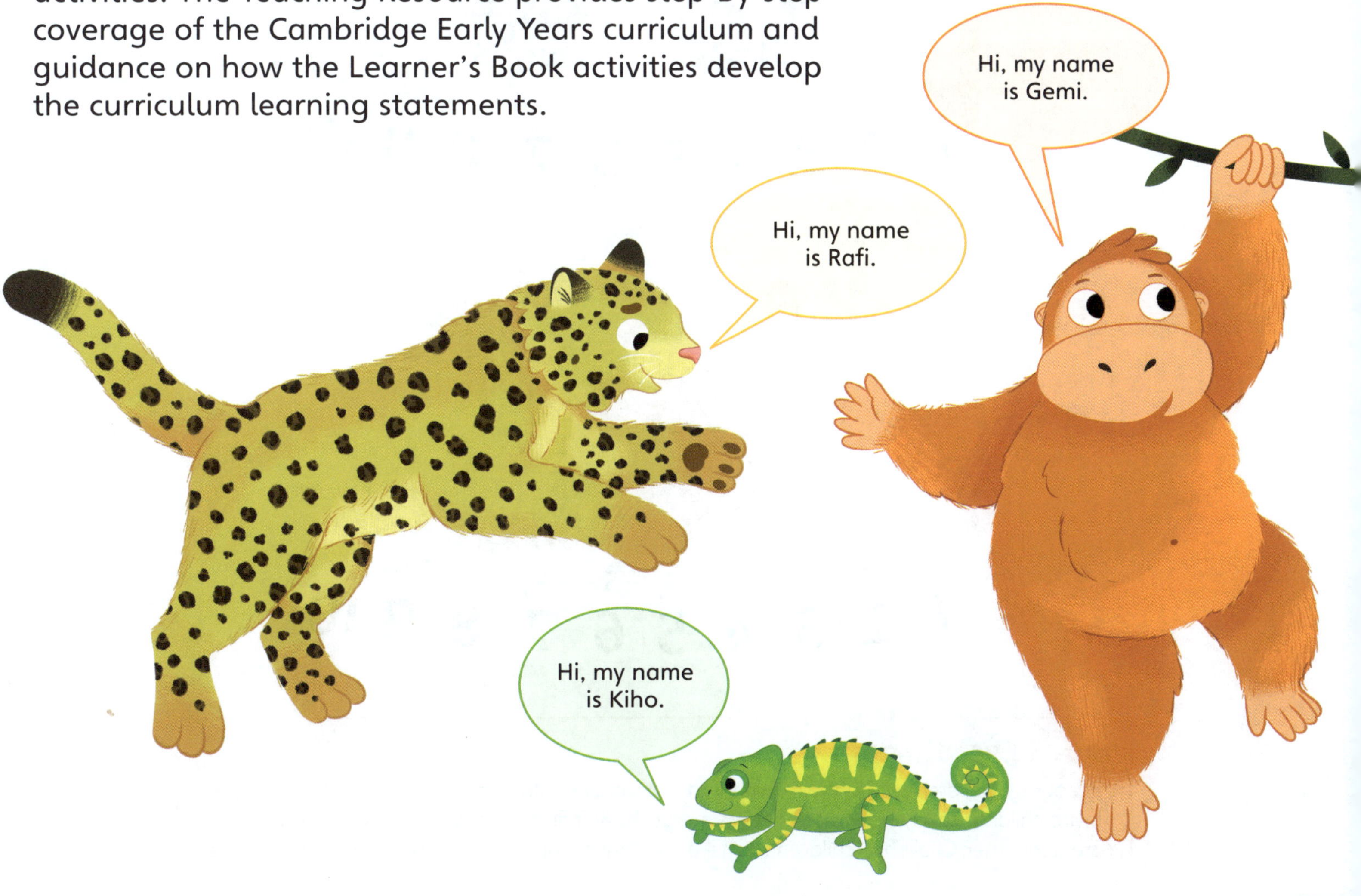

Hi, my name is Mia.

Find us on the front covers doing lots of fun activities.

Hi, my name is Gemi.

Hi, my name is Rafi.

Hi, my name is Kiho.

Block 3: Caring for ourselves and the world

Number pairs for 10

Count and colour.

How many fingers are up?
How many are folded down?
Colour both numbers on each washing line.

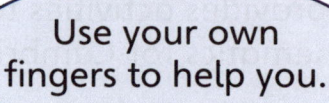
Use your own fingers to help you.

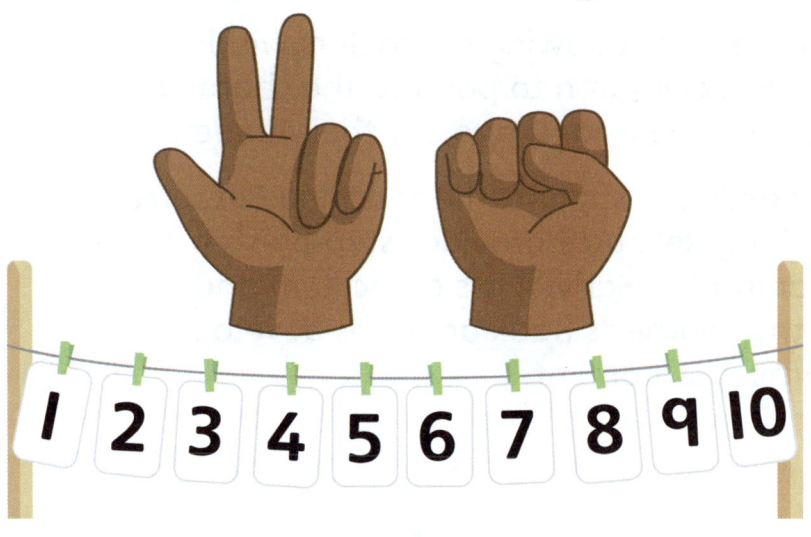

For practitioners
Encourage children to use their own hands for visual reinforcement of number pairs to ten. Invite children to say how many fingers are up, how many are down and how many there are altogether. Challenge children to make different number pairs to ten using their fingers.

Ten horses

Draw and say.

Farmer Kahina wants seven horses on one side of the field and three horses on the other side. Draw a line across the field to help her.

| 1 | 2 | 3 | 4 | 5 | 6 | 7 | 8 | 9 | 10 |

For practitioners

Encourage children to count and check they have the correct number of horses in each part of the field. Invite them to say how many horses are on each side of the field, and how many there are altogether. They can use the number track for support. Challenge children to think of other ways they could group the horses using different number pairs to ten.

Making ten

Colour and say.

Colour 6 red spots and 4 blue spots.

Try putting counters on the spots first, then colour.

Colour 2 red spots and 8 blue spots.

For practitioners

Once children have coloured the spots, invite them to say how many spots are in each colour and how many there are altogether. Challenge children to compare their Hungarian ten frames with a partner. How are they the same or different?

Staircases

Colour and say.

Continue the pattern.
Colour the next step to show 12.

Remember that 12 is equal to 10 and 2 more.

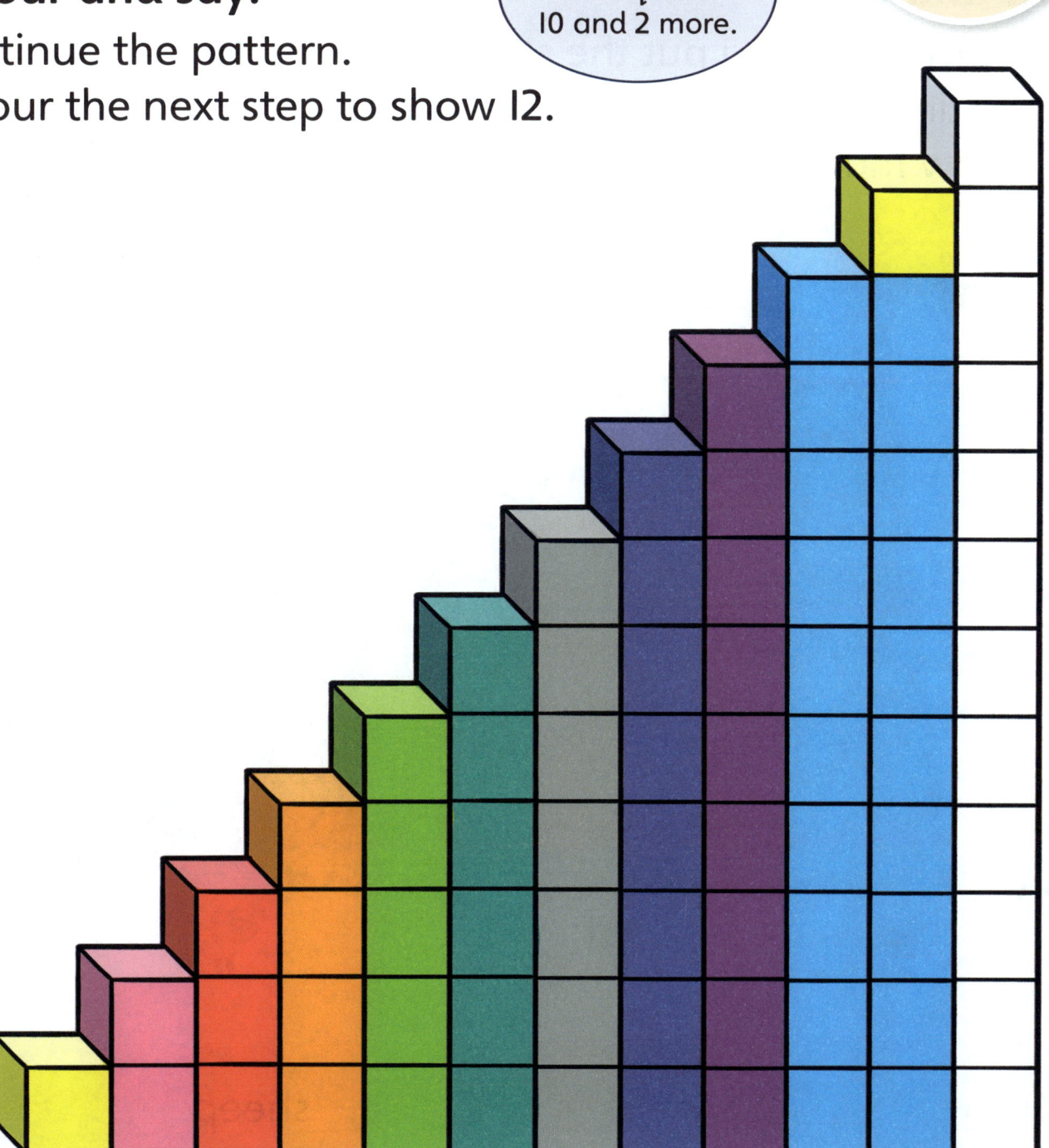

For practitioners
Invite children to say how many cubes are in each column. Children could build their own staircase using coloured cubes. Focus on building a staircase of ten and two more to show how 12 is 10 and 2. Challenge children to continue building a staircase up to 20.

Fields of sheep

Draw and write.

Help Farmer Kahina put the sheep in the fields. Draw a line from each sheep to a field, then write how many sheep are in each field.

_____ sheep   _____ sheep

For practitioners

Children can choose how many of the 12 sheep to put into each field. Invite children to say how many animals there are in each field and how many there are altogether. Give children toy animals and a green field (e.g., green paper or fabric) to try solving this practically. Challenge children to split the 12 sheep up between the fields in another way.

16 bugs

Colour and say.

Colour some bugs in yellow.
Colour some bugs in red.
Write how many of each colour there are.

> Remember the last number you count is also the total.

yellow bugs: _____   red bugs: _____

For practitioners

Give children sets of two different coloured counters so they can try this activity practically first.
Then invite children to say how many red bugs and yellow bugs they have coloured, and how many there are altogether.
Challenge children to find other ways of decomposing 16, thinking about how they could colour the bugs differently.

Adding machine

Add and say.

There are 10 blue balls and 4 green balls in the adding machine. Find out how many balls there are altogether.

Use the number line to help you find the total number of balls.

10 balls and 4 balls is equal to ☐ balls.

☐ + ☐ = ☐

For practitioners

Look at the adding machine with children and discuss how it might work – where the balls go in and where they come out. Ask children to explain how they worked out the total number of balls. If they counted all of them, show them how to count on from 10 on the number line to find the total number of balls.

Number line adding

Mark and add.

Use the number line to find how many grapes there are altogether.

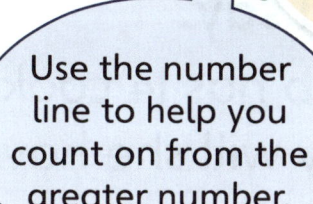

Use the number line to help you count on from the greater number.

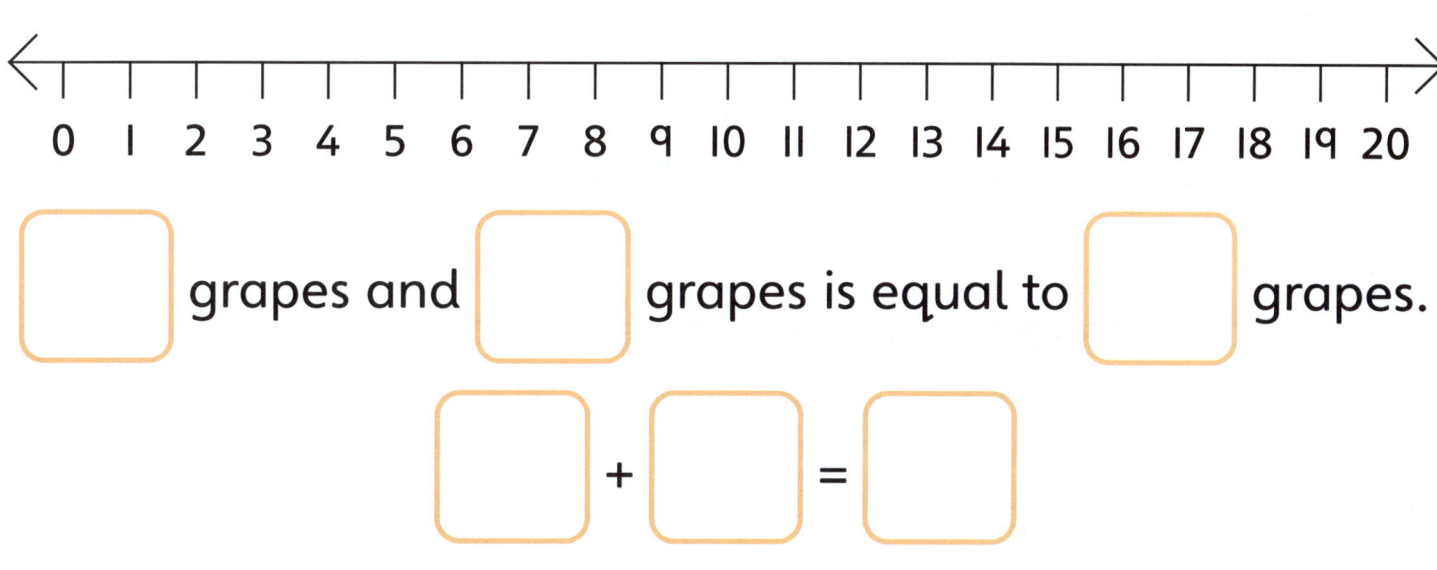

☐ grapes and ☐ grapes is equal to ☐ grapes.

☐ + ☐ = ☐

For practitioners

Encourage children to find and circle the number 12 and to then count on 3, either as 3 single jumps of 1 or as 1 jump of 3. Invite children to say their number sentence. Challenge children to add different quantities together using another number line (e.g., 14 and 3) and record the calculation using the model above.

Taking away

Write and say.

Cookie Cub has 14 cookies.
How many will she have if she eats 4?

Use the number line to help you take away 4.

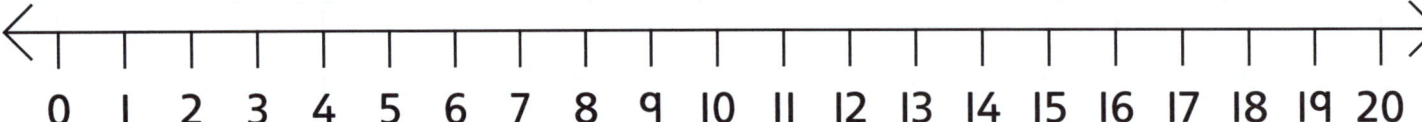

14 cookies take away 4 cookies is equal to ☐.

For practitioners
Ask children *Will you have more or fewer cookies if you take four away?* Invite children to say the completed number sentence. Challenge children to take away a different number of cookies (e.g., 14 – 6) and record the calculation using the model above.

Find the difference

Use the number line to help you find the difference in the number of cookies.

Write and say.

What is the difference between the number of cookies Cookie Cub has and the number Gemi has?

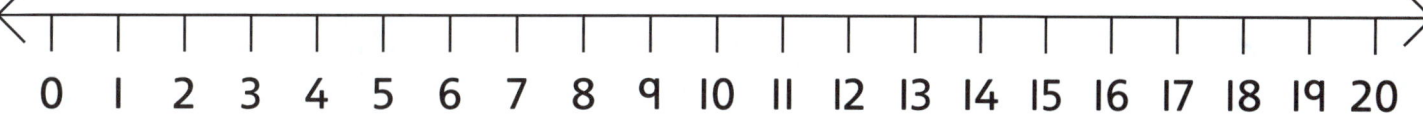

The difference between ☐ cookies and ☐ cookies is ☐ cookies.

☐ − ☐ = ☐

For practitioners

Help children explore counting back from 15 to 9 and counting up from 9 to 15 to find out the answer. Give children lots of practice finding the difference using both methods and salt dough cookies or counters.

Bug subtraction stories

Mark and say.

There are 13 bugs. Tell a story about 13 − 7. Complete the number sentence.

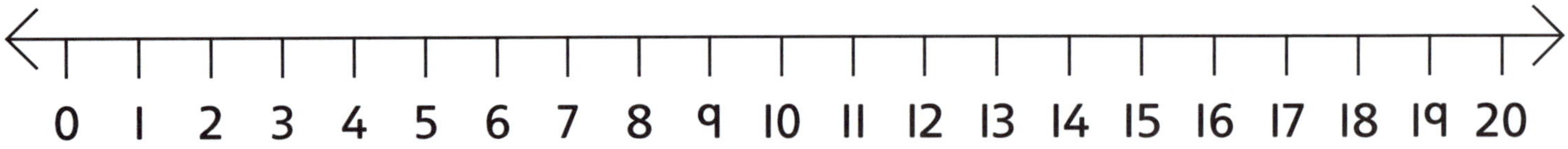

Use the number line to help you.

For practitioners
Children could work practically first, using counters as bugs. Ask *What kind of story is it — taking away or finding the difference? Did you use counting up or counting back to find the answer?* Challenge children to use both strategies for the same calculation.

Estimating how many
Estimate and circle.

Look at the pictures with a partner. Tell each other what you notice.

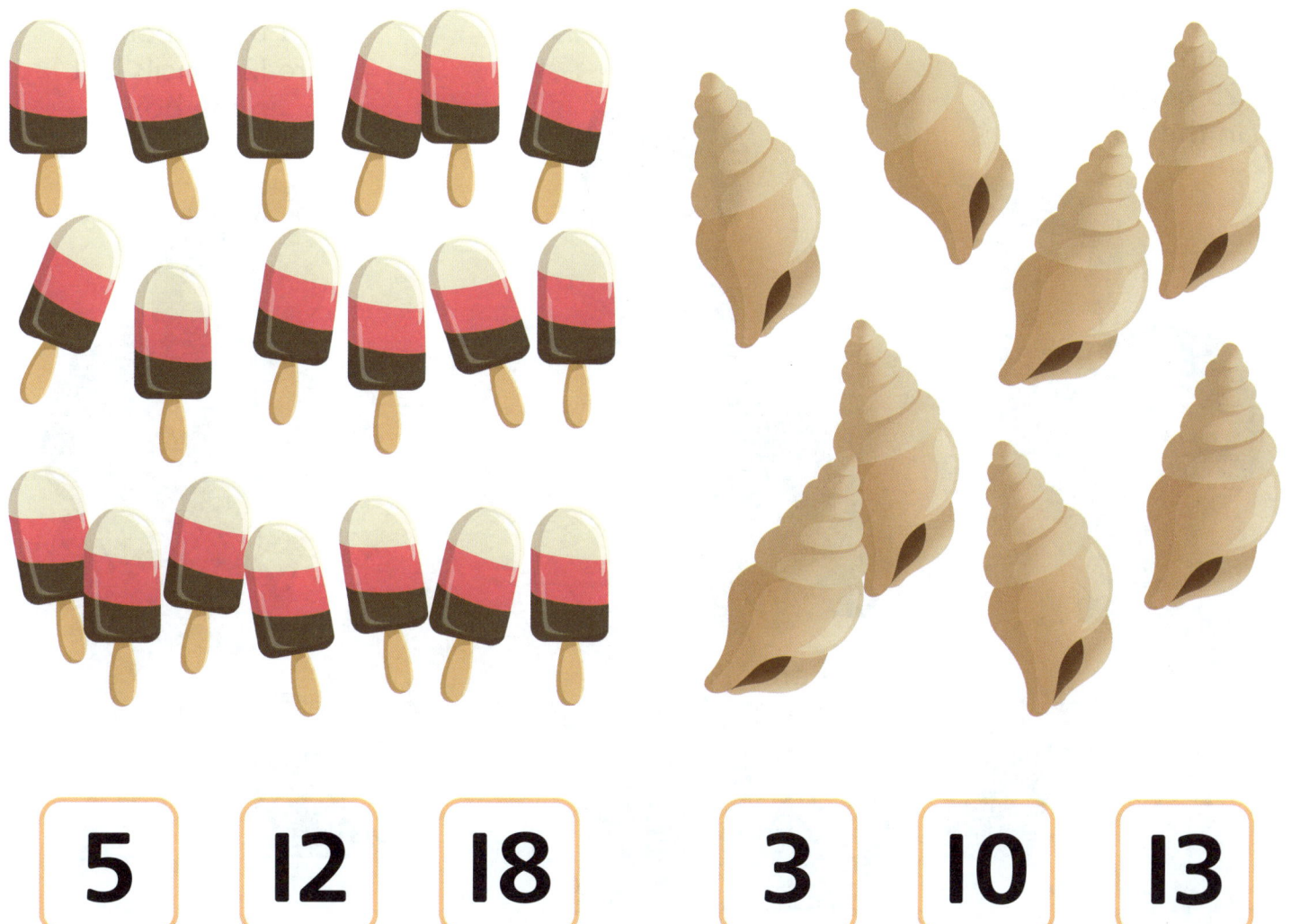

| 5 | 12 | 18 | | 3 | 10 | 13 |

For practitioners
Encourage children to look at the pictures and estimate the correct number of items rather than counting them. Challenge children to make up their own collection of objects, show them to a partner and ask them to estimate how many there are.

Estimating pencils

Estimate, tick and check.

The children just opened a new box of 20 pencils.
How many pencils are left in the box?
Tick the estimate you think is closest.

For practitioners
Encourage children to look at the picture and discuss the ideas in the speech bubbles, then tick the one they think is the best estimate. Challenge children to then calculate the answer and compare this with their estimate.

Party time

Estimate and circle.

There are 19 children at Mishti's party, but 4 are leaving. Estimate how many children will be left at the party.

Think, don't count.

I think there will be 9 children left.

I think there will be 23 children left.

I think there will be 14 children left.

For practitioners
Discuss the picture and speech bubbles with children, encouraging them to think and reason, rather than counting the number of children that are left. Challenge children to estimate how many children there would be at the party if another four children left.

Block 4 # Then and now

Shape sort
Sort.

Check each shape to see which basket it belongs in.

flat faces

curved faces

For practitioners
Give children a set of 3D shapes to explore and sort first. Children then draw lines to sort the shapes into the correct baskets, and discuss if there is a shape which belongs in both baskets (cylinder). Challenge children to name or draw some other objects for each basket.

2D shapes

Find and colour all the shapes with 4 straight sides in blue. Then move on to the shapes with 1 curved side.

Colour and say.

Colour the shapes with 4 straight sides in `blue`.
Colour the shapes with 1 curved side in `yellow`.

For practitioners
Encourage children to look at the shapes and count the straight sides on each before colouring them in. Challenge children to name the blue and yellow shapes and the shapes which are not coloured.

Carroll diagram: 3 straight sides

Look for all the shapes with 3 straight sides first.

Sort.

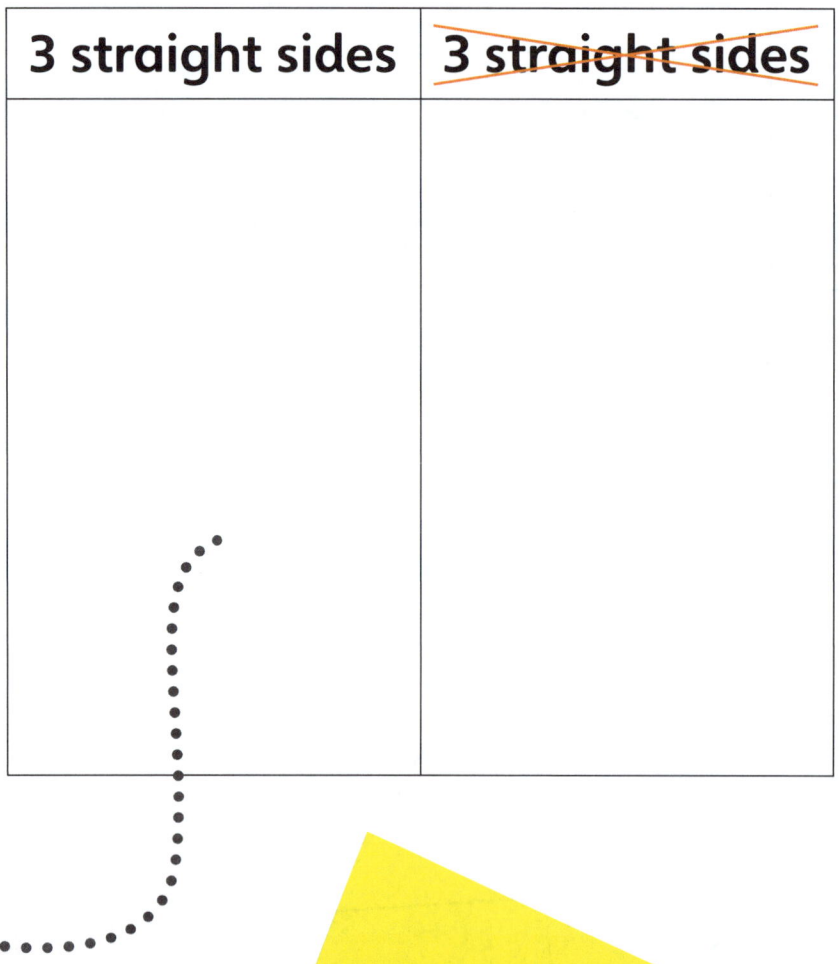

For practitioners
Encourage children to count the number of straight sides on each shape before drawing a line to put it in the correct place in the Carroll diagram. Challenge children to name the shapes that have 3 straight sides and the shapes which do not, and to describe another property of each shape.

Carroll diagram: 1 curved side

Draw shapes.

Draw shapes in one column first, then in the second column.

Curved side	~~Curved side~~

For practitioners
Give children a selection of 2D shapes to look at to help them decide which shapes to draw in each part of the Carroll diagram. Challenge children to draw at least three different shapes in each column.

Venn diagram: buttons

Sort.

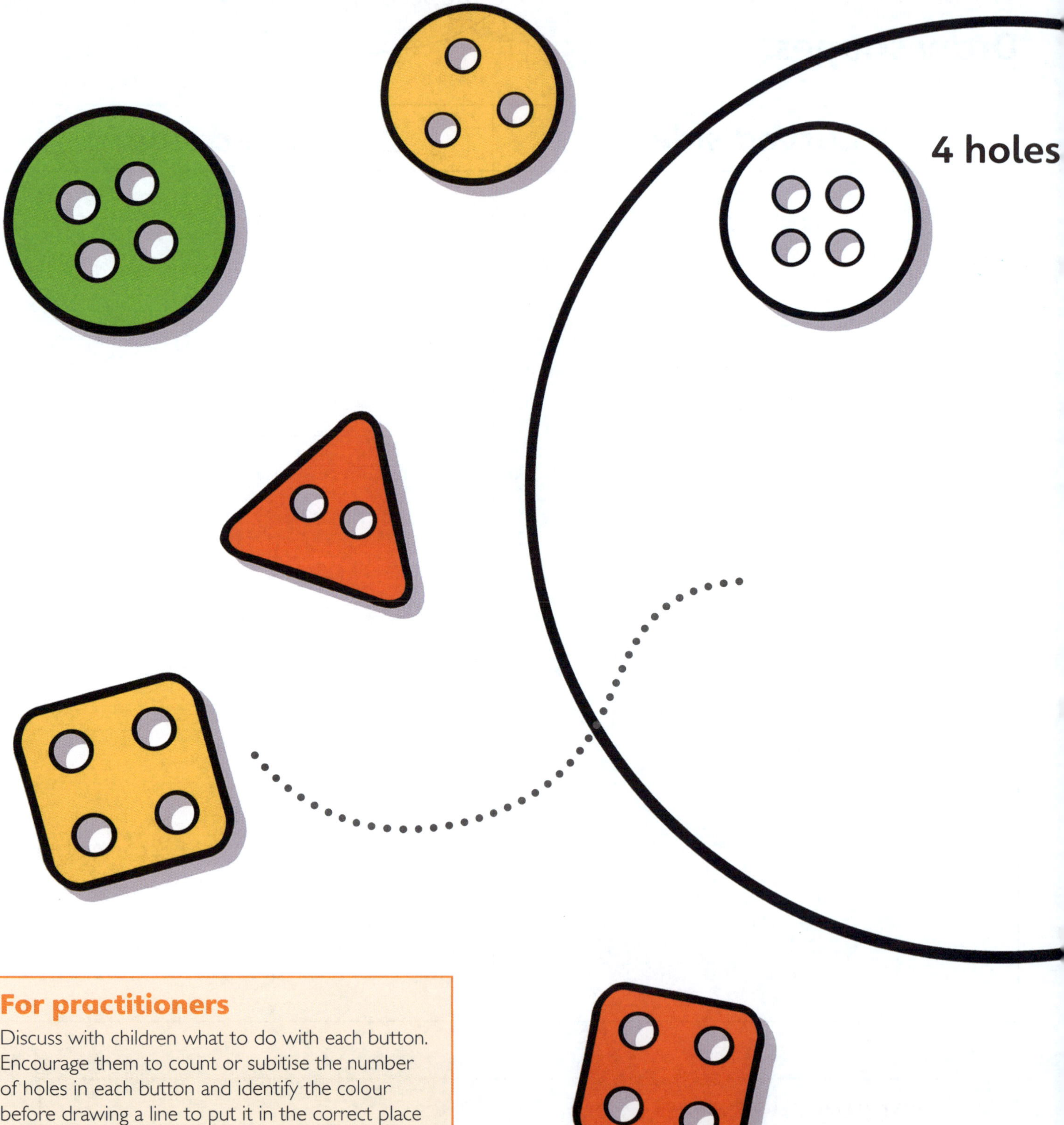

4 holes

For practitioners
Discuss with children what to do with each button. Encourage them to count or subitise the number of holes in each button and identify the colour before drawing a line to put it in the correct place in the Venn diagram. Give children a selection of buttons to explore and group in their own way.

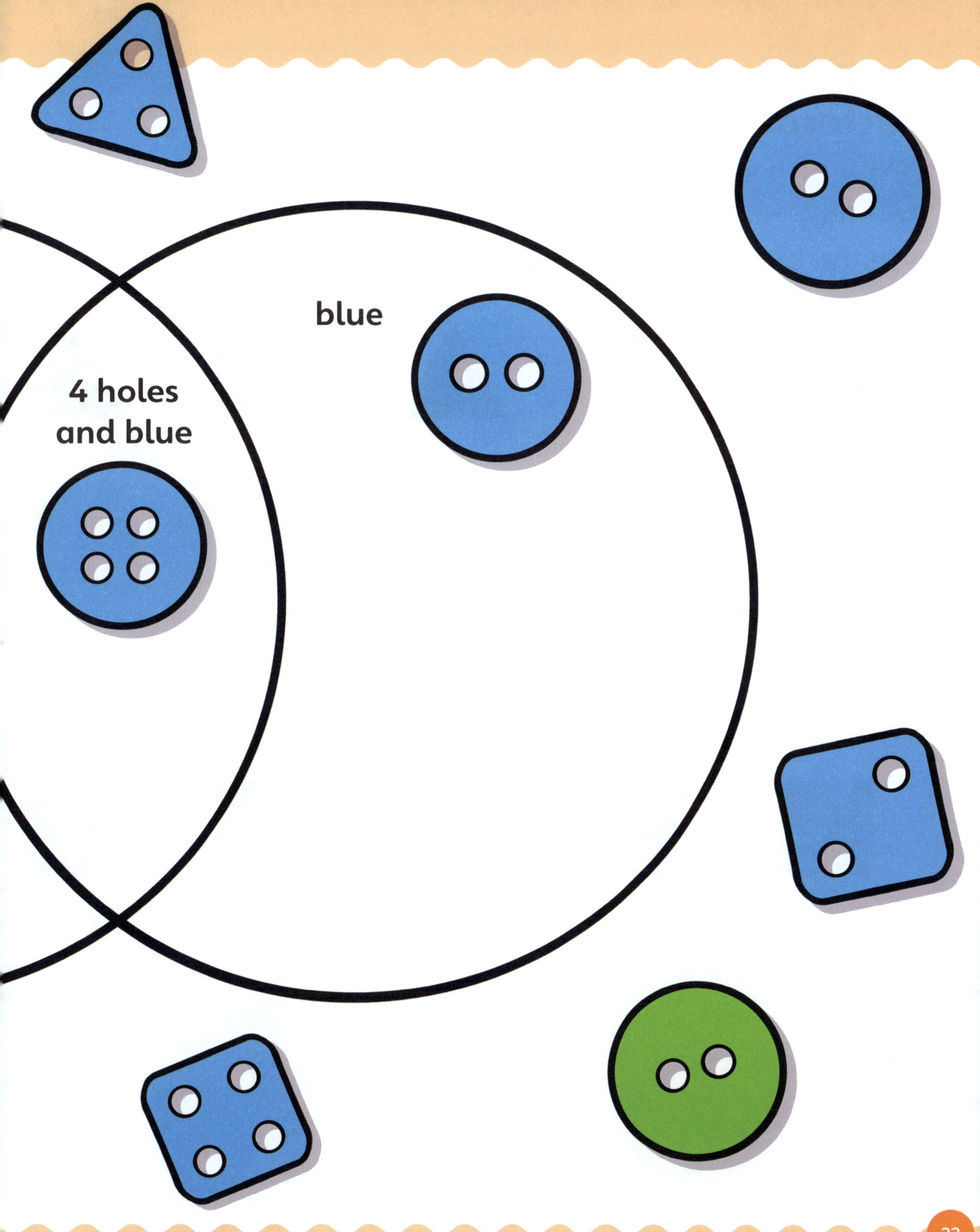

Patterns

Draw and say.

Continue the patterns.
Use the blank strip to make your own pattern.

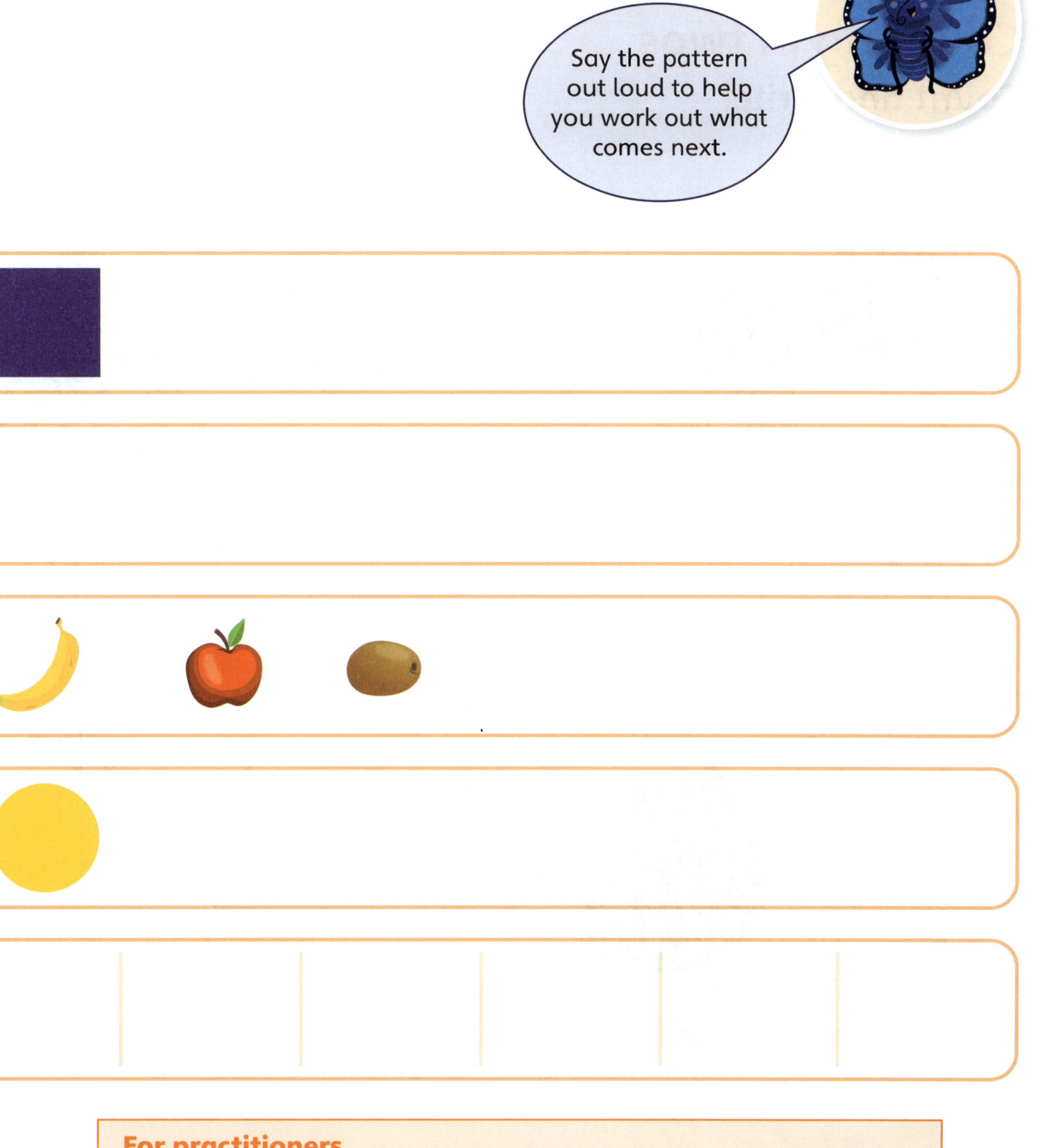

For practitioners
Draw a circle around the unit of repeat (e.g., triangle square in pattern 1) to support children to continue the pattern. Challenge children to make a pattern with at least three units of repeat, then change one object to make a deliberate mistake. Ask another child to find and correct the mistake.

Counting in twos

Count and write.

Position

Look, say and draw.

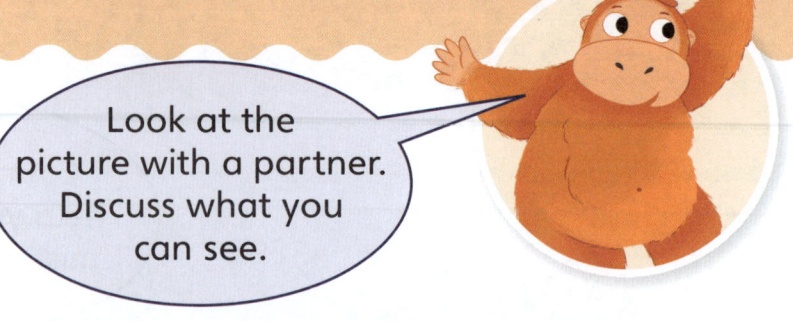

Look at the picture with a partner. Discuss what you can see.

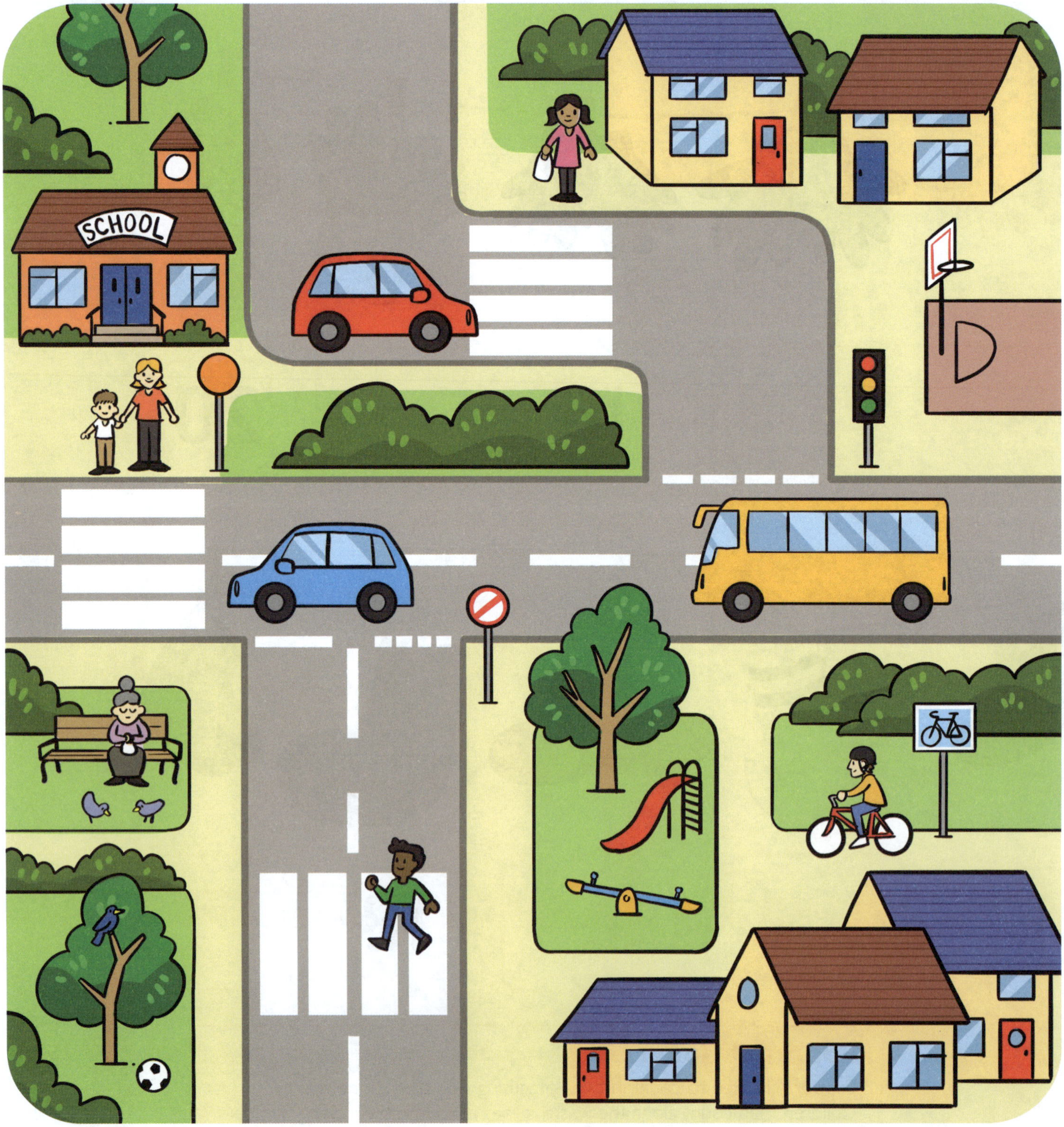
SCHOOL

What is **between** the tree 🌳 and the see-saw 🛝 ?

What is to the **right** of the school 🏫 ?

What is to the **left** of this sign 🚲 ?

What is **below** this tree 🌳 ?

For practitioners
Encourage children to look at the picture and describe some of the people and objects in it using positional words such as *between*, *above*, *below*, *left*, *right*, *around*. Children then read the questions and draw pictures to answer them.

Treasure map

Follow and say.

Talk about what you see on the way to the treasure.

Start at the star.

For practitioners
Encourage children to talk through the features on the map, using directional language to describe their position. For example, *the bridge is to the left of the castle*. Invite children to follow the paths with their finger and choose the paths that will take them to the treasure. Challenge children to draw their own treasure map and decide where the treasure is hidden.

Recording a route

Draw and say.

Draw a map of the route from your classroom to the school gate.

Try to imagine walking along the route you are describing.

For practitioners
Encourage children to use landmarks along their route for support. Some children may find it helpful to record their route as they walk it. Suggest other suitable routes for children to describe to a partner, for example, the route from where a child is standing to the classroom door.

Acknowledgements

The authors and publishers acknowledge the following sources of copyright material and are grateful for the permissions granted.
While every effort has been made, it has not always been possible to identify the sources of all the material used, or to trace all copyright holders.
If any omissions are brought to our notice, we will be happy to include the appropriate acknowledgements on reprinting.

Thanks to the following artists at Beehive Illustration:
Laura Arias, Keri Green, Michelle McGovern, Joe Wilkins.

Cover characters by Becky Davies (The Bright Agency)